SAMCAM
The Hero From Winslow Street

JANENE OLIPHANT

SamCam
Copyright © 2024 by Janene Oliphant

ISBN: 979-8991517911 (sc)
ISBN: 979-8991517928 (e)

All rights reserved. No part of this publication may be reproduced, distributed, or transmitted in any form or by any means, including photocopying, recording, or other electronic or mechanical methods, without the prior written permission of the publisher and/or the author, except in the case of brief quotations embodied in critical reviews and other noncommercial uses permitted by copyright law.

The views expressed in this book are solely those of the author and do not necessarily reflect the views of the publisher, and the publisher hereby disclaims any responsibility for them.

Riverview Press

info@riverview-press.com
www.riverview-press.com

TABLE OF CONTENTS

Chapter 1	About Sam	1
Chapter 2	A Brilliant Idea	5
Chapter 3	A Good Sign	7
Chapter 4	Linda Brown	11
Chapter 5	Miss Dove	15
Chapter 6	A Piece of Art	18
Chapter 7	Middleton Park	20
Chapter 8	Hero Nurse	22
Chapter 9	Let's Roll	25
Chapter 10	Such Wonderful Things	28
Chapter 11	A Very Special Thank You	31
Chapter 12	Busy Boy	34
Chapter 13	Hidden Surprises	36
Chapter 14	The Secret Message	38
Chapter 15	Food and Friendship	42
Chapter 16	Just a Trim, Please	46
Chapter 17	Eleventy Billion Dollars	49
Chapter 18	Two Congratulations	53
Chapter 19	Mr. Avery Has an Idea	55
Chapter 20	Picture Taking Day	57
Chapter 21	Mum's the Word	61
Chapter 22	A Little Hero	63
Chapter 23	The Very, Very, Very Best Day Ever!	**67**
Chapter 24	A Family Portrait	70
Dedications and Acknowledgements		72

CHAPTER 1
ABOUT SAM

The door of the house on Winslow Street opened and Sam Cameron tiptoed out onto the front porch. The floor boards creaked a bit as he walked over to the steps and plopped down. It was early in the day so he tried to move quietly. He didn't want to wake Annie, his mother, or Sandy Patty, his little sister.

It was nice sitting outside in the cool morning air, listening to the quiet. This was Sam's thinking time. And he had a lot to think about. Lately the world seemed to be spinning out of control. Something dangerous called COVID-19 had brought everything to a stand-still. Even during the school year, Middleton Elementary School had closed and he and his friends had to stay home. Now it was summer and he still couldn't go anywhere. So, Sam tried extra hard to come up with ideas to help his mother around the house. She was a single mom and needed all the help she could get. Why, he had even gone out of his way to entertain Sandy Patty by playing dolls with her, for goodness's sake! And that wasn't the most fun thing to do.

Sam looked up at the sky and squinted his eyes against the brightening sun. He had seen dozens of mornings like this, but it wasn't the same as it had been before the virus. He often wondered how the rest of the world was handling things. It showed on TV how a lot of people were stuck at home without work, or school, or having fun with their friends. It felt like living in a science fiction movie. The evening news reported people wearing masks over their faces. That was to keep germs away from themselves and to stop from spreading the virus to others. It was because of the virus that Sam's mother couldn't go to work anymore. Her job at The Sunflower Florist Shoppe wasn't considered an essential business so her boss had closed it. It sure didn't take long for Sam to realize that his mother was troubled about money. She looked worried all the time and there was never very much food in the cupboards or refrigerator.

The virus had brought some changes to the Cameron family routine. For one thing, they didn't have to be up at six-thirty to get ready for school and work. Sam was still an early riser which made it hard waiting for brunch. Brunch was the smashed together word Sam used to describe both breakfast and lunch. It came at ten-thirty when the family each had a bowl of cereal. There were some mornings when Sam's stomach growled so loud with hunger that he had trouble waiting to eat. Their new luppertime (Sandy Patty had combined the words lunch and suppertime) was at five o'clock. That usually consisted of a hotdog, or a lunchmeat sandwich, or maybe soup, with a banana or apple. Sometimes there would be a cookie for dessert. Sometimes. Sam remembered when they ate three meals a day but he figured it wasn't a big deal now. He didn't have school recesses or P.E. anymore. He didn't even play hard enough in his own yard to work up much of an appetite. He wasn't losing any weight but he wasn't gaining any either.

He *had* noticed that his mother was getting thinner. He thought maybe she was on a diet or something. Sam also noticed how long her hair was getting. Just the day before, he'd told her how pretty it looked and was surprised to see her eyes fill with tears.

Yes, there had been changes, but some things were still the same. Sam continued to think that the old Victorian three-story house on Winslow Street was the most interesting place to live. He loved his family's home which was the entire first floor apartment, Number 101. It had shiny wood floors and a yellow and white kitchen. The fireplace in the living room was cozy on cold winter nights. Sam loved his bedroom with the blue quilt and red curtains. And he and Sandy Patty spent hours playing outside on the wooden wrap-around porch. It was all good.

One of their neighbors, Miss Dove Corwin, lived on the second floor in apartment Number 201. It was a delightful space with lots of flowery curtains and furniture. She'd been a music teacher before retiring. Sam often heard her playing her piano and singing in a high, sweet voice.

Another neighbor, Chris Maille, lived next to Miss Dove in Number 202. He'd served in the army for ten years, but now worked as a milkman by day and took college classes online at night. Since he worked for a dairy company, his work was essential. Sam's mother said he was one of the lucky ones. Everyone liked Chris, especially Sandy Patty. He was the reason they were able to get milk for their cereal. He brought them a new carton every few days.

Old John Avery lived on the top floor in Number 301. He was very quiet and kept to himself. Sam felt sorry for him. Recently something very bad had happened. Mr. Avery had just lost his roommate brother, Noah, from COVID-19. Sam knew exactly how Mr. Avery felt. A few years before, Sam's dad had become ill with cancer and passed away. The little Cameron family had been heartbroken. Annie tried to explain it to the children at the time, but Sandy Patty was too little to understand. She just knew she wanted her daddy back. Now, she couldn't remember too much about her daddy, but she remembered a lot about Noah. He was someone who had been a very talented artist. That was his job…creating amazing paintings.

Noah Avery would haul his easel down the two flights of stairs and set up his equipment in the backyard gazebo. Sam often peeked out from behind his living room curtains and watched when he worked outside. After Noah had finished several pieces of art, his business manager, Tim Tabor, would come collect them and hold auctions at the Middleton Convention Hall. People came from miles around to buy an Avery painting. Sam was fascinated by all the beautiful colors and textures that the talented artist created. Sometimes he wished he could just step into the pictures that appeared on the canvases. Even today, he often thought how much he missed his neighbor. And his dad. But now those sad things were in the past and life had calmed down a bit.

Yes, having interesting neighbors was a very good thing about the house on Winslow Street. However, they all found themselves living with the threat of the COVID-19 virus that had now spread around the entire world.

* * *

CHAPTER 2
A BRILLIANT IDEA

Whew! It was getting hot sitting on the porch. Sam got up and went back into the house. He turned on the TV, keeping the sound low. The local news was running an interesting story about posters and signs that people were making to put in their yards. He sat down to watch.

"Wow!" Sam whispered as he read the messages.

THANK YOU, HEROES and *BLESS YOU FOR CARING* and *WE ARE THANKFUL FOR YOU*

Something stirred inside him. He liked how health workers, firemen, policemen, store clerks, and others were being honored.

I want to tell them, too, he thought. *Maybe I can make a sign.*

Suddenly, Sam had a brilliant idea! Each apartment was assigned a storage room down in the basement. He remembered the leftover cans of paint down there that his dad had used on the lawn chairs, porch railing, and various projects around the house. He darted for the basement stairs off the apartment hall entryway. Oh! It felt strange. The only time he went to the dark, spooky storage room was when his mother had him take things downstairs that she didn't need upstairs.

He hustled down the steps and looked around for the paint. First, he came across a box of old toys that he and Sandy Patty had outgrown. He reminded himself to tell his mother that it would be okay to give them to Goodwill. But for now, the Goodwill store was closed, just like The Sunflower Florist Shoppe. Next, he found some boxes that held his dad's old clothing. Sam sucked in his breath. He'd forgotten they were down there. Suits and ties, flannel shirts and blue jeans. And an old work shirt that had dried paint splashed all over it. Sam picked up the shirt and held it to his nose. He could still smell his dad! Or, at least the aftershave he always wore. He felt a lump form in his throat as he put all the clothing back into the boxes. All, that is, but the work shirt.

Looking around, he finally spotted a shelf filled with paint cans and brushes. He gathered them together and put them in a sturdy cardboard box. But wait! He still needed something to paint on. In the corner of the storage room, he saw a tin sign with two metal stakes for legs. They had used it for last summer's yard sale and a STUFF FOR SALE paper was still taped to it. Sam pulled it out from behind some boxes and lumbered up the basement stairs with his supplies.

* * *

CHAPTER 3
A GOOD SIGN

His mother and little sister were awake and sitting at the table when he went into the kitchen.

"Good morning!" Annie said with a smile. "I saw the basement door open and wondered if you went down there to explore." She put her hands on her hips. "Or," she teased her son, "perhaps you decided to clean our storage room." She noticed all the things he was carrying. "Hmmm, are you going to make something? Looks interesting."

Sam set his load aside and sat down to eat the cereal she'd fixed for him.

"Would you mind if I use some of this stuff?" he asked. "I saw on TV that people are making signs to say thanks to the heroes who are working hard to help others. You know, with the virus and all. I think I'd like to try to paint a sign, too. Would it be okay?"

Annie's eyes filled with tears. When Sam saw this, he wondered *Am I saying something wrong? I'm always making her cry!*

To his surprise she walked over, leaned down, and hugged him tight.

"Yes, Sam," she said quietly, "you may use anything you find down there to make as many signs as you want." She straightened up. "Maybe Sandy Patty can help. That would be a nice project for the two of you."

His sister ferociously nodded her head up and down.

"I can help! I really need something to keep my hands busy."

Sam and Annie burst out laughing. That was certainly true!

The children wasted no time in heading to the front yard. It took Sandy Patty two trips to lug out all the brushes and paint. Sam carried the metal sign out and laid it on the grass. Before he opened the paint cans, he put his dad's old work shirt on over his T-shirt.

"Whatcha gonna write?" Sandy Patty asked her brother, when she saw him pull a black marker from his pocket.

"Haven't decided yet. Something simple, but something good!"

He thought for a while, then carefully began to mark on the sign. He wrote out some lovely letters and a very unique border around all the edges. When he finished, he drew a row of hearts across the bottom.

"Sam, we gots white paint and yellow paint and black paint, and some red, too! The red will be great for the hearts, don't ya think?"

"You bet! How about I paint the letters and you can help fill in the hearts?"

The morning passed quickly. Their sign was turning out even better than they could have imagined! The children were so busy working they hadn't noticed that a man was standing on the front porch, watching them.

"What are you two doing?"

Both children jumped in surprise.

"Wow, Mr. Avery, you scared the heck out of us!" Sam said in a shaky voice.

"I sure didn't mean to do that," the old man said, smiling. "Just wondered what you were up to. It looks to me like you're doing something important."

"We're paintin'. Sam wants to say thanks to the heroes that are helping our country."

"I see that. And what a fine job you're doing. Both of you." Mr. Avery paused. "It's good to see someone painting again. My brother loved painting outside, too."

"I know," Sam said. "I liked it when he worked in the gazebo. I'd stand at the window and watch him for hours. One day, I just went right out and introduced myself to him. He was a very nice man."

Mr. Avery looked startled. "That's right! He told me about that. It was when he first met you. You told him your name was Samuel Anthony Cameron. He said your name was too long for such a little guy so he was always going to think of you as SamCam. Did he ever tell you that?"

"No, he didn't. SamCam, huh. But you know what? I kinda like it!"

Mr. Avery's face creased into a big grin and he began to laugh. That felt good! It had been a while since he had really laughed. "You're right. I kind of like it, too."

Sam glanced back at his finished sign. He dipped a small brush into the can of black paint. In the lower right corner, he wrote something. SamCam.

The children started to pick up the sign and Mr. Avery stepped forward to help them. They all worked together to set it straight in the middle of their yard. About that time, Annie came outside to check on her children's progress.

"How's it coming, kids? Oh, hello Mr. Avery. How are you?" She walked down the porch steps and looked at the sign.

"Oh, just watching some budding artists do an amazing job," he answered.

She studied the painting in wonder. "I should say so! Actually, kids," she said slowly, "I'd say you did a *perfect* job."

The old man took a longer look at the sign. She was right. It *was* perfect.

"You know something, SamCam? Your work here is quite exceptional." He thought for a moment. "I think you have real artistic talent. Do you draw or paint?"

"I've wanted to try ever since I watched Noah working on his paintings. But I never thought I could do anything like that. I figured you had to be a special kind of person. Like your brother."

The old man looked at Annie. "Mrs. Cameron, would you be okay with me giving some art supplies to your son?" Mr. Avery cleared his throat. "You know my brother was an artist and so much of his stuff is just going to waste. If SamCam is interested in trying something new, he's welcome to it."

Annie turned towards Sam. He nodded in excitement.

"That's very nice of you, Mr. Avery. What a generous thing to do."

"That settles that! I'll bring some things down to your apartment later."

He hurried back into the house with a spring in his step. If the boy could help others, then, by golly, he would help the boy!

After he left Annie looked at her son and raised one eyebrow. "SamCam?"

* * *

CHAPTER 4
LINDA BROWN

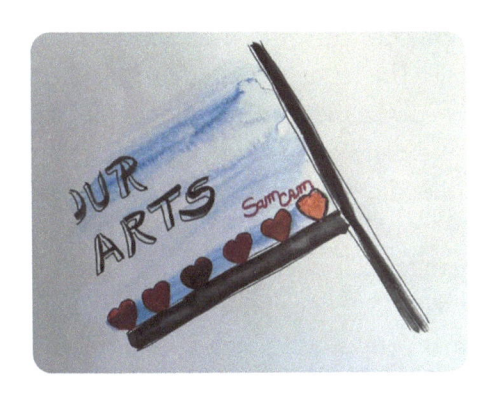

"Helloo! Is anyone home?"

Annie stopped wiping the kitchen counter and looked at the children.

"Is someone outside?" she asked. "What in the world …?"

Sam and Sandy Patty jumped up from the table and ran to the window. There was a woman standing on the sidewalk just beyond their front yard. She spotted the children and waved.

"Hi, there," she called out. "I have a question about this." She pointed to the sign that Sam had made.

"Let's go check this out," Annie said. "Remember, stay by me. Masks on. Keep near the house."

"Why, hellooo!" the woman said happily when the Camerons appeared on the front steps.

"Can we help you?" Annie asked, politely.

"I'm Linda Brown. I live three houses down from you. I was just walking up to Miller's Food Mart and saw your sign. I love it!"

She bent over and read the words that Sam had written.

TO AMERICA'S HEROES
THANK YOU FROM THE BOTTOM OF OUR HEARTS

"Someone did a beautiful job painting this sign. I'm simply amazed." She put her hands to her cheeks, trying to contain her excitement. "The lettering is perfect and the lovely hearts go so cleverly with the message. I'd like to put one in my yard. My sister is a nurse and *she's* a hero, too. May I ask who did it?"

"My brudder did it. But I helped a little," Sandy Patty said, proudly. "Here he is."

The woman looked at the small boy in surprise. She really didn't know what to say.

"Young man, you must be quite the artist to paint such a professional looking sign."

She thought for a minute and then said, "I'm serious about getting something for my yard. Could I hire you to make one for me? Oh, I'd supply the paint and blank sign. And I can pay you…say twenty-five dollars for your work. Would that be fair?"

Sam looked at his mother. She smiled and shrugged.

"It's up to you. That would give you something to do. And, it'd be a nice thing for the neighborhood."

The woman clapped her hands happily when Sam nodded at her.

"My husband and I will bring the supplies by later. Is it alright if we just put them on your front porch? We'll knock three times to signal you and then leave."

So, Sam and Linda Brown had a deal.

As she turned to go, Linda paused. "If you want to make mine the same as yours, that's fine. But if you want to make it different, I trust you. I have a feeling that you can come up with lots of good ideas for honoring our heroes. Um, I see yours is signed by SamCam. Is that your name?"

"My neighbor gave me that nickname," Sam said, shyly. "It's short for Samuel Cameron."

"Oh, my goodness! That is so cool!" the lady exclaimed. "Well, SamCam, be sure to sign my piece, too. I'll be happy to show off your work."

Later, that evening, Sam heard someone on the porch. There were three quick knocks on the door, and then the sounds of people walking away. Linda Brown and her husband had delivered the supplies. The family hurried out to see what they'd left.

"Look," Sandy Patty exclaimed, "she brought all kinds of paint and a bare-naked sign. I think she wrote you a letter, too. Read it!"

Sam picked up an envelope that was taped to a paint can and pulled out a paper.

> *SamCam, here is some stuff that you can use. I don't need this paint anymore. You are welcome to keep it all. You might be asked to do more signs. My phone number is below. Would you call me when you are finished? I put $25 in the envelope for your time.*
>
> *Thanks, Linda Brown*

Sam pulled the money out and looked at his mother in amazement. He'd never held that much money in his whole life. He tucked it back inside the envelope and handed it to her.

"Would you put this away? I'll think about what to do with it when the job is done."

Then he got down to business. He found a pad of paper, got a pencil, and curled up on the sofa. He began to write down some ideas. Suddenly, his mind was filled with all kinds of designs. He experimented with different lettering styles and an assortment of borders. He made several sketches of pictures.

A whole bunch of messages came to him and he quickly jotted them all down. Sam worked until Annie reminded him that it was time to shower before bedtime. He reluctantly put the pencil and pad down on the coffee table and headed for the bathroom.

Annie glanced down, picked up the pad, and flipped through the pages. But when she saw what Sam had been working on, she was shocked! Why, Sam had come up with some brilliant sayings. Details in his sample drawings were jaw-dropping. One sketch of a face looked so real and so familiar, but who was it? As Annie stared into the person's eyes, it came to her who it looked like!

She began to cry. But this kind of crying felt good. She realized that Sam was doing something very, very important. Pride for her little boy overwhelmed her. She didn't know how, or when, or even why, but she felt he was going to make a big difference in the lives of others.

* * *

CHAPTER 5
MISS DOVE

The next day there was a knock at the Camerons' door. Annie opened it to find Miss Dove from Number 201, standing in the hallway.

"Hi, Annie," Miss Dove said softly. She was holding a covered plate. "I hope I'm not disturbing you. I made a batch of cinnamon rolls. There's too many for just me, so I'm sharing with everyone in the building." She set the plate on the floor and stepped back.

Annie looked at the flowery print mask that Miss Dove was wearing and grinned. That lady liked flowers as much as *she* did. She bent down and picked up the plate.

"Oh, Miss Dove, how lovely! This is very thoughtful of you," she said. "And it's so nice to see you. We haven't actually visited with any friends in a long time."

The old lady smiled shyly behind the mask and turned to leave.

"Wait!" Annie reached into her pocket and pulled out her own mask. "Would you feel comfortable sitting on the porch for a while? I just made a fresh pot of coffee. Maybe we could enjoy some of your rolls with it. I'll move the rocking chairs six feet apart and we can still have a nice chat."

Miss Dove nodded. Now she had a radiant smile on her face behind the mask.

Annie quickly got two mugs of coffee from the kitchen and joined her on the porch.

Sam was busy in the front yard, putting a base coat of paint on Linda Brown's sign. He had chosen a bold wine color for the background. He wanted the message and designs to really stand out against it. His head bobbed up and he gave Miss Dove and his mother a little wave. Then back to work he went. Sandy Patty sat near him, playing with her Lolly Polly doll. She felt it was her job to keep an eye on her brother's work.

"Kids, look what Miss Dove brought us!" Annie called out. "Some cinnamon rolls that she baked herself. She's sharing them with us. Isn't that nice?"

The children sniffed the wonderful aroma in the air and bounced to their feet.

"Miss Dove, they smell so good. Thank you, thank you, thank you!" Sam declared.

Sandy Patty's tummy rumbled. She could use a snack right about now. It was going to be a while before luppertime.

"Sam, would you please get some milk for you and your sister?" Annie asked. He dashed into the house and returned with two full glasses. The children each took a big roll and sat down on the porch swing. This was fun. It was good to have a visitor.

"Sam, may I ask what project you're working on? It looks fascinating," Miss Dove said.

"I'm painting a thank you," he told her. "Have you seen on TV that people are making yard signs?" he asked. "You know, to honor all the workers who are helping others."

"Oh my, yes," she replied. "But haven't you already posted a message right there by the sidewalk?" She got up, walked down the porch steps, and went to take a closer look at Sam's sign. "What a nice piece of work. Did you make this one, too?"

"Yup. That one is for our front yard. I mean, ours, and yours, and Mr. Avery's, and Chris's front yard. A lady who lives down Winslow Street saw it and asked if she could hire me to paint one for her. That's what I'm working on. I sure got a lot of ideas of what I'd like to say."

The sweet old lady leaned toward the sign, pushed her glasses down her nose, and looked at the writing in the lower right corner. "SamCam. Hmmm. Is that you?"

Sam blushed. "I just found out that Mr. Avery's brother, Noah, called me that. It's short for Samuel Cameron. I thought it might be nice to sign my picture with that nickname."

"Why, that's a very good idea. Noah must have recognized that you were going to be an artist, just like him. And, sometimes, an artist can use an artistic name. I approve!"

***

CHAPTER 6
A PIECE OF ART

The next week Sam telephoned Linda Brown to let her know that he had finished her project. She was absolutely thrilled that he had done it so quickly.

"Oh, good! I'll bring my husband by this evening to pick it up. I'm so excited to be getting a piece of your art to honor my sister. See you later!"

It was going to be several hours before the Browns came to his house. Until then there was nothing to do and frankly, Sam was just plain bored. He tried to think of something to keep himself occupied. Sandy Patty was taking a nap. His mother was sewing some new face masks that she planned to give to Miss Dove, Mr. Avery, and Chris.

Hmmm… he thought idly, *it's kinda funny that Linda said my signs were pieces of art. I wonder what she meant by that.*

Suddenly, Sam remembered something. Art! He had been so busy he hadn't taken the time to look at the easel, paints, canvases, and brushes that Mr. Avery had given him. He dashed into the living room and found the box of supplies sitting by the coffee table. That's when he had a wonderful thought. He'd try using Noah's things to paint a picture for his mother.

After finding a canvas that looked just right, Sam coated it with a layer of something called gesso. He wasn't sure what it did, but he remembered Noah doing it so it must be important. While the canvas was drying, he pulled out some tubes of paint. He had seen on TV how artists squeezed a dab of each color into the dips of a plastic paint palette. He recalled that paint could be mixed together to make entirely new colors. This was going to be interesting!

He found a package of sketching pencils among the supplies. Noah had always started by marking out an idea on the canvas.

Soon. Soon he would have something pretty to give to his mother. And he knew exactly what she'd like.

* * *

CHAPTER 7
MIDDLETON PARK

"Sandy Patty! Sam! It's time to eat."

The children came running. Wow, the kitchen smelled absolutely wonderful.

"We're having grilled cheese sandwiches tonight," Annie said cheerfully. "And there's cupcakes for dessert."

Sam looked at his luscious sandwich. They hadn't had that in a long time. He loved grilled cheese. But cupcakes, too? This was a real treat.

"Chris thought we might like a change, so he brought us and Miss Dove and Mr. Avery some packages of cheese from the dairy store. He gets a big employee discount, so it didn't cost us very much. And Miss Dove had some extra flour she didn't need, so I made cupcakes for everyone."

Sandy Patty wriggled on her chair in excitement. Sam grinned. He hadn't felt this good in a long time. First, he had spent an afternoon of pure joy as he worked on his mother's painting. Then, knowing that the Browns would be coming soon was exciting. And now a wonderful luppertime. Life was good!

Annie had a very happy look on her face.

"Oh, and I have another surprise for you two. After the Browns take their sign, we're going down the street to Middleton Park. You guys need some exercise and fresh air."

Sandy Patty looked confused.

"Why do we gets to go to the playground? I thought we couldn't go nowhere. Has the virus gone away?"

"No, but I heard back from the city council that we can go to the park in the evenings. It seems that no one has been using it. So, I asked about it and they said that we could go. We'll pretend it's our very own private playground. What do you think of that?"

Oh boy oh boy oh boy! Sam thought to himself. *This is the best day ever. I'm so full of happiness, I feel like I could just explode!*

After eating, the children helped wash and dry the dishes. Then Annie put some cupcakes into three plastic containers. The plan was to take them to their neighbors before heading to the park.

* * *

CHAPTER 8
HERO NURSE

"Hellooo! Is anyone home?"

It was Linda Brown and her husband.

Sam and Annie had already taken the sign out and leaned it against the porch steps. Now Sam was anxious to find out what Linda thought of it. After all, she had paid him twenty-five dollars for it. That was a lot of money. He didn't want to disappoint her.

Sandy Patty opened the front door and they all looked out. Everyone watched as the Browns stood in front of the thank you sign that Sam had made especially for them. But they weren't saying a single word. They just stood there staring at it.

Sam cringed.

"Mom, something's wrong," he whispered. "I don't think they like it at all!"

Annie waited patiently, smiling. She knew what was going on. She knew what the Browns were thinking.

Mr. Brown leaned down and studied the sign more closely, while Linda began to cry. Finally, she controlled herself, gave a big sigh, and looked right at Sam.

"How old are you?" she asked.

Sam was surprised at the question. Why did she want to know that?

"I'm just asking because I can't believe that someone as young as you is so talented." She turned to her husband. He smiled and nodded in agreement as he read the words.

NURSES STAND BY US EVERY DAY
LET'S STAND BY THEM
THANK YOU TO THESE BRAVE HEROES

"I can hardly take it all in. The lettering is beautiful. And the picture! This is such an amazing piece of art."

Suddenly, Mr. Brown pointed at the sign.

"Uh…Dear, wipe the tears from your eyes. You might want to look again. Do you see what I see?"

Linda leaned closer to the sign and gasped!

Behind the words, there were wispy white clouds floating across a glowing wine-colored sky. Sam had painted the face of a nurse below the written message. She was wearing a blue papery cap on her head and a bit of her blue papery medical gown was showing. Her hand was lifted to remove her white mask. She wore a stethoscope around her neck that appeared so real it made you want to reach out and touch it. She looked tired as if she had just worked a very long shift. But what made Linda Brown gasp was the woman's face above the mask. It looked just like her!

By now, Sam was very nervous. "I…I…hoped you'd like it. I tried real hard. I wasn't sure how to paint the face, so I just made it look like you." Sam waited uncomfortably for an answer but Linda Brown seemed unable to speak.

"I'll…I'll give you your money back," he stammered. "It's okay. And Mom can help me take the sign away."

Linda Brown took a step toward him, then remembered to stay back.

"Oh, Sam, my sister is my twin! You made it look just like her, too. This is so cool! I can never thank you enough." She began to laugh. "And don't you dare mention taking this sign away from me. I'll treasure it long after this stupid virus is gone. After all, my sister is a true hero. Her work with all the sick patients at the hospital is exhausting but she never complains."

Before leaving, Linda Brown checked to see if Sam had signed his work. There it was, in the lower right corner. SamCam. She gave him the thumbs up.

When the Browns got to the sidewalk, Sam remembered something.

"Linda?" he called out.

"Yes, Sam?" she replied.

"I'm nine."

* * *

CHAPTER 9
LET'S ROLL

What an exciting day! As soon as the Browns left, the Camerons all clumped together for a group hug.

"You did it, Sam, you did it!" exclaimed Sandy Patty. "You made that lady really happy with your sign. It was bootiful."

"Yes, Son," Annie agreed, "you certainly did an amazing job. The Browns were very satisfied with your work." She paused. "But can you tell me something? Where's your talent coming from? I've never seen anyone do such perfect work without any previous practice. Or lessons!"

"I don't know, Mom. It just seems to come naturally. I never dreamed I could paint like this. I guess Noah is looking down and helping me. And Dad, too. He must know that I wear his shirt whenever I paint."

"Maybe, Sam. Maybe," Annie said wistfully.

Suddenly, Sandy Patty pulled away from the other two. "Hey, let's deliver those cupcakes and then go to the park. I can't wait any longer!"

Annie stepped back into their apartment, grabbed the plastic containers and up the stairs they went. They stopped at Miss Dove's first. Sam let his little sister knock.

"Hi there," the little girl blurted out as soon as the door opened. "We brought you some cupcakes. And they're dullicious."

"Oh my!" said Miss Dove. "They certainly look delicious."

"After we take some to the other neighbors, we gets to go to the park. The city conshell said we could. We're gonna have the whole playground to ourselves."

Annie nodded at Miss Dove's puzzled look.

"I checked with the city *council* and found out that it was okay. Nobody is using Middleton Park so they said we could go and enjoy it." She looked at Miss Dove and smiled. "Would you like to go, too? It would be something different for a change. And we would love to have you with us."

The old lady's face lit up with joy. "Why, I'd like that. I'll change into my walking shoes while you deliver the rest of your cupcakes. I'll be ready in a jiffy."

As Miss Dove shut her door, they heard her whistling cheerfully.

The next stop was at Number 202. Sam knocked this time. When Chris opened his door, Sandy Patty pushed the container into his hands.

"Hi! We brought you some cupcakes and want to know if you can go to the park with us."

Chris looked at Annie. Her face reddened in embarrassment.

"Sorry, Chris. We made treats for everyone in the building. When we delivered Miss Dove's, she agreed to go to the park with us. You know, something different to do. I guess my daughter thinks everyone in the building would like to go. We don't want to bother you. I'm sure you have things to do."

Chris threw back his head and laughed. "Actually, I'm not doing anything important." He looked down at Sandy Patty's sweet face and then back at Annie. "I think a walk in the park with a pretty girl would just about make my evening perfect." He patted the little girl's head." Sure, I'll go with you."

Then the Camerons went up the stairs to Number 301. Annie knocked and the door opened.

"Hello, Mr. Avery. We brought you some cupcakes. We hope you enjoy them."

Sandy Patty pushed in front of her mother. "We're goin' down to the park. And we want to know if you'll go with us. Miss Dove is goin' and Chris is goin'. It sure would be nice if you came, too."

Annie just went with it this time. "Would you care to go for a walk in the park? I found out that the children can play there in the evenings. The others said they wouldn't mind going with us. But don't feel like you have to."

Mr. Avery didn't have to give it a second thought. He reached over to a small table just inside his apartment door, picked up his baseball cap and put it on.

"Let's roll!"

* * *

CHAPTER 10
SUCH WONDERFUL THINGS

A little parade was making its way along the sidewalk beside Winslow Street. First came Annie, holding Sandy Patty's hand. Next came Sam. Miss Dove followed, with Mr. Avery and Chris bringing up the rear. They were careful to stay spaced apart while still having a good time. They laughed and called out to each other as they walked along. Everyone was proudly wearing their new red, white, and blue face masks that Annie had sewn.

"We look like we're members of a special American club!" Sam announced to the others.

Suddenly, Sandy Patty stopped in her tracks. "Oooh!" she squealed, pointing. "There's the bootiful sign you made, Sam."

They all came to a halt by a white fence surrounding a pretty little yard. It was the house three doors down from home. This was where Linda Brown lived. As they viewed Sam's work. Miss Dove, Mr. Avery, and Chris were stunned when they saw the incredible art that he had created.

Just then, Linda came out of her house and saw them. "Hellooo everybody!" She seemed quite excited. "SamCam, I have the most unbelievable news to share with you."

She moved a bit closer to the sidewalk. "I took a picture of this sign with my phone and sent it to my twin sister. She loved it! Anyway, she showed it to Dr. Phillips, the head medical director. And, guess what? *He* loved it! Now he wants to know if he can hire you to make a special thank you painting to display inside St. Luke's Hospital. He said he would pay you fifty dollars for your work. Are you interested?"

Sam looked at his mother for approval. She smiled and nodded her head.

"I'd like that, Linda. It'll be another fun project," Sam said quietly.

So, Linda told Sam that she would arrange to have the hospital deliver the supplies to his house the next day. She also told him about a few simple requests that the director had asked for. Sam nodded his head. He knew he could do the job and shivered with joy at the thought.

His friends let him know how happy they were for him. Mr. Avery was delighted that there was another request for a SamCam sign. Chris put his hand in the air and gave the little boy a high-five. . .from a distance.

"If I dared to, I'd give you a great big hug!" Miss Dove said happily.

This day was getting better and better. Now off for some more fun.

When they got to the park, Sandy Patty dashed for the swing set. Miss Dove and Mr. Avery went for a stroll around the big water fountain. Sam joined his little sister. He was going to swing as high as the sky and let the wind blow in his face. It was wonderful being at the park again. Annie and Chris made their way over to the duck pond and sat down on a bench surrounded by flowers. It was the perfect place to keep an eye on the children.

A gentle breeze was spreading the fragrance of roses all around them.

"I'll bet you miss this since the florist shop closed," Chris said, sniffing the air.

Annie nodded. "I *do* miss it. But I'm just grateful for important moments like this. My children are happy and healthy. I'm spending a gorgeous evening with good people that I think of as friends." She laughed, looking right at Chris. "And we had wonderful grilled cheese sandwiches tonight."

She glanced over at the children swinging back and forth. "I *am* a bit confused about what is happening right now. My little son has developed a talent for painting exceptional pieces of art. That's something none of us could have ever imagined happening. I can't explain it. I don't think *he* can explain it. It's simply something that makes him happy which makes me happy for him. Especially considering how things are going on in the world."

Later, as the sun began to set, the American Club headed home. Everyone had enjoyed their time at the park and decided that they would do it again soon.

When they got to the big old house, Mr. Avery announced that he would like to do some grilling on Saturday night. Would they all like to meet in the backyard near the gazebo? He'd make some of his special hamburgers for everyone. They all agreed, delighted for another good thing to look forward to.

But for now, Sam's mind was already spinning with ideas for the hospital's sign. Tomorrow he would get busy and do something really wonderful.

* * *

CHAPTER 11
A VERY SPECIAL THANK YOU

It took Sam seventeen days to finish the hospital sign. For one thing, it was larger than his other pieces. There were also some special details that he wanted to paint and he wasn't about to rush the process. When it was done, he showed it to his mother. Sam was a bit worried when she didn't say anything for a long time. Finally, she turned to him and gave him the huge hug that Miss Dove hadn't been able to give him.

"Sam," she said in a husky voice, "this is truly remarkable. The hospital will be thrilled to get this. Trust me." Together, they pulled the heavy sign out to the front porch. Just then, Chris came walking up the sidewalk.

"Hold up, you two! I'll help you with that."

The three of them carried the painting down the stairs and propped it up against the house. Chris stepped back to see what Sam had done. He looked first at the little boy, and then at Annie. He raised his eyebrows in surprise. "Honestly, Sam, did you really do this all by yourself?"

"Yup!" Sam said, grinning.

The painting showed a big brick building with *St. Luke's Hospital* marked across its front. An American flag was flying from the rooftop. Sam had painted a vivid pinkish-gold sunset. A group of doctors and nurses wearing scrubs and masks stood in front of the hospital. Each person was painted in fine detail. Chris looked closer into the faces Sam had created. He saw younger versions of Miss Dove and Mr. Avery. He saw Annie's face, and Linda Brown's, and others he didn't recognize. In the front row—he saw himself.

AMERICAN TOUGH
STRONG * CARING
THANK YOU TO THESE HEROES

"Wow! We need to get Miss Dove and Mr. Avery down here now!" Chris said, shaking his head. "They've got to see this."

Sam shrugged and dashed into the house to get the others. Chris looked at Annie in disbelief.

"Have you called that hospital guy yet?" Chris said slowly. "I can't wait to see his face when he gets a look at it!"

Two hours later, Dr. Phillips, the head medical director, drove up in a van. He had brought another man to help him load the sign. By this time, Miss Dove and Mr. Avery sat waiting in the porch rocking chairs. Chris was leaning against the railing and Annie was on the porch swing with the children. Linda Brown and her husband had also showed up. They stood patiently on the sidewalk. Linda's sister had called her and said that the director was on his way. Several people who had been driving by saw the large painting and stopped to get a better look.

Dr. Phillips got out of his van and walked slowly across the front lawn. He couldn't seem to take his eyes off the sign.

When he finally did, he looked at Sam. "Young man," he said, clearing his throat, "is this the kind of work you do?" He looked down at the check he held in his hand. "Uh, I'm not going to pay fifty dollars for this!"

Everyone watched in surprise as the man tore up the payment. Then something strange happened. Dr. Phillips reached into his shirt pocket and pulled out his checkbook. He scribbled something on a blank check, tore it out, and laid it on the grass.

"I think *this* is more appropriate. You have outdone yourself. Thank you!"

Then he leaned closer to look at the lower right corner of the painting. He got a big smile on his face. There it was. SamCam. "Perfect!" he declared. "This is a signed treasure!"

As soon as the men left, Sandy Patty scampered down the porch steps and picked up Sam's check. "Gee, it sure gots a bunch of zeroes!" she said as she handed it to him.

"Five hundred dollars," Sam read aloud. "*Wait!* Mom, does this say *five hundred* dollars?" Sam was thunderstruck. His hands were shaking. He couldn't believe what he was seeing.

Annie nodded her head, laughing with joy. Everyone around them began to clap.

"I think, SamCam," Mr. Avery said proudly, "you are now considered a professional artist."

* * *

CHAPTER 12
BUSY BOY

Sam was very busy from then on. Soon, every house on Winslow Street had one of his thank you signs in their yard. All the neighbors wanted one. People from all over town began driving down Winslow Street just to see the beautiful pictures that a little artist called SamCam had created. They began to order signs, too.

Sam absolutely loved what he was doing and could finish a project quickly. Some people just wanted words on their sign, and some wanted a picture to honor a certain part of the workforce. When asked what he charged, he checked with his mother first. She had become aware of what everyone thought they were worth and apparently everyone thought they were worth a lot! Every buyer *knew* they were getting a special treasure and were eager to have a SamCam painting.

Since he had never had any money before, Annie helped him open an account at the bank and he deposited most of his earnings at the drive-up window. The rest he took in cash. He had plans for it.

* * *

CHAPTER 13
HIDDEN SURPRISES

Sam got up slowly and stretched his legs. He'd been sitting on the gazebo floor working longer than he should have. Mr. Avery was cooking out this evening and would be coming soon to start the grill. Sam needed to get moving. He smiled. He'd heard some talk about having chicken tonight.

No one else in the house knew that there were some wonderful surprises hidden in the back of the gazebo. He'd worked on them in his spare time but there was still a bit of work to do on the smallest one. Then it would be ready for tonight, too.

The surprise he was most eager to give was meant for his mother. Sam was very satisfied with the way it had turned out. But he wasn't waiting until later. He decided to put that special piece in the house and just let her find it. So, after slipping into the kitchen and placing it on the table, he snuck out the front door. Sandy Patty was busy dressing, undressing, and redressing

Lolly Polly as she sat on the porch swing. She glanced up at her brother.

"Whatcha doin'?"

He walked past his sister and over by the sidewalk that faced the house. He sat down on the grass and propped up the small canvas. After laying out a small collection of paint supplies, Sam went to work putting a few finishing touches on the picture. "Nothing," he said absent-mindedly. Sandy Patty got up and started across the lawn toward him, but he held up one hand. "Stop! I don't want anyone to see this yet. Okay?"

Sandy Patty rolled her eyes and went back to the porch. She knew he could get a bit grouchy when he was painting. Besides, she had more important things to think about. Like deciding if it was too hot today to put a winter coat on her doll, or just let her be in her swimsuit.

* * *

CHAPTER 14
THE SECRET MESSAGE

Annie sat down and picked up Sam's painting. She'd found it when she set a basket of laundry on the kitchen table and prepared to fold towels. At first, she was caught up in its beauty and colors. Then, she'd discovered the little secret that was woven into the design. She was lost in thought when there was a knock at the door. It was Chris with two big cartons of ice cream.

Hi, Annie," he said. "Look what I brought you. I didn't know if the kids like chocolate or vanilla, so I got both!" He held up the cartons.

Annie gave him a worried smile. "Oh, Chris, you shouldn't have! That was very kind of you. Come on in and I'll get you your money."

Chris laughed. "Um . . . this is on me. I've always liked ice cream on warm summer days. I thought maybe Sam and Sandy Patty would, too."

"No, Chris," she said. "It was a nice thing to do, but I'm still going to pay you. I want to."

She went over to the red rooster cookie jar. Annie held her breath, hoping that there was enough money in it. This is where she always put some cash to pay him for the milk, or cheese, or butter that he brought her from the dairy store. But she was pretty sure that she had used it all up. If the jar was empty, she would be so embarrassed. She lifted the lid, slipped in one hand, and felt around. *Please, please, please let there be enough to buy at least one carton*! she thought. Crackle! There was a rustling noise. Something was in the jar! Annie pulled her hand out and looked in. Why, there was a pile of money in there. Ones, fives, tens, and several twenty-dollar bills. Where had they come from? Then, she knew.

Carefully, she pulled out the appropriate amount of money and held it out to Chris. However, he just waved it away with his hand.

"Nope. I got this for the kids. If you try to pay me, I'll just have to take it home. And there's no way I can eat all this by myself. So, you're just going to have to accept it this time."

Before Annie could say anything more, he noticed the painting lying on the table. "I see your little artist has been doing some more great work. Mind if I look at it?"

"I wish you would. There's something in this one that's different from all his others. Look closely. Do you see it, too?"

Chris pulled out a kitchen chair and sat down. He picked up the painting and held it gingerly in his hands as if holding something fragile.

Sam had painted three sunflowers standing up in a big glass canning jar. The colors were so vibrant! Golden petals and dark brown centers, with pale-green stems standing in shimmering clear water. The details were exact, and there was even a life-like bumble bee sitting on one of the flowers. Chris was amazed that the stunning art had actually been done by a nine-year old boy. It was an incredibly beautiful painting. He studied it carefully and wondered what Annie wanted him to see. She'd said there was something different on the canvas but he couldn't quite figure it out.

She leaned over his shoulder and pointed at one of the flowers. Then he saw it. Hidden within the picture were a few words. He looked up and stared at her.

"I love you."

Annie began to laugh. "You got it! You see it! Can you imagine how that little boy managed to slip that into his work? It's genius."

Chris looked back at the sunflowers and softly repeated, "I love you." He carefully laid the painting on the table. "Hmmm—that's one special boy you've got. That's for sure." He got up and headed for the door.

"Oh, say," he said snapping his fingers. "Don't forget that Mr. Avery is grilling in the backyard later. I'm bringing my special coleslaw. I think Miss Dove made potato salad. So, bring the kids and your appetite. It's going to be a great evening."

"Guess what?" Annie answered. "I'll bring the ice cream!"

As soon as the door shut behind Chris, she gave a shout. "Samuel Anthony Cameron, march yourself out to this kitchen. Now!"

Sam opened his bedroom door and looked out. "Are you okay? What's going on?"

Annie pointed to the cookie jar. "Do you know what I found in there?" she asked sternly.

"I think so," Sam said carefully.

"Money. That's what I found. Did you put it in there?"

Sam nodded. "I want to help you," he replied. "I don't have anything that I need to buy 'cause you always take good care of me. I know grown-ups have bills to pay."

"*You* earned that money. I just can't take it."

"But it would make *me* happy. It isn't that I'm giving it to you. I'm *sharing* it with you."

Annie sighed. "I don't know what to say except thank you. But, more importantly, I want to thank you for the painting. I saw the special message you spelled out in it. That means all the world to me."

"I was hoping you'd see it," he said happily. "That was something that just came to me so I hid it in your flowers." He kissed her cheek. "I also wanted to help you remember The Sunflower Florist Shoppe and know that someday you get to go back to that pretty place. Then, maybe things will be normal again."

* * *

CHAPTER 15
FOOD AND FRIENDSHIP

The sun was going down and the air was cooling off. The children were excited to join all the others by the gazebo for yet another wonderful meal. Mr. Avery had indeed grilled chicken. Yes, Miss Dove brought potato salad, and Chris had made his special coleslaw. Annie provided the ice cream, plus a pan of buttery corn on the cob. Linda Brown had a huge garden behind her small house, and would frequently bring the Camerons lots of special things. Tomatoes, peas, carrots, and now sweet corn.

Sam was looking forward to the meal with their friends but he was also excited about something he was about to do.

As soon as everyone was done eating, Sandy Patty collected their paper plates. Annie made sure that they all had refills of ice tea before she sat back down in her lawn chair. Sam took the trash from his sister and carried it into the house.

Annie and Miss Dove chatted about a cooking show they had both seen on TV. Then Mr. Avery asked Chris about his college classes.

"They're going well," Chris told the old man. "I've just about completed everything for my degree in business. It's tougher learning online than it was in the classroom at Middleton College. But someday maybe I'll be able to work in an office at the dairy company instead of delivering milk."

"Good for you, young man!" Miss Dove said. "An education can open up a lot of opportunities for you."

Annie smiled. "We are all so proud of the hard work you're doing, Chris. Good job!" Chris looked at Annie. It sure meant a lot to him that his friends were glad for him.

Just then Sam appeared in the doorway of the gazebo. No one had paid any attention when he'd sneaked in there while they talked. But now they watched as he carried out some canvases. He walked over to everyone and stood facing them.

"While we're all together, I'd like to give each of you guys something."

Sam took the smallest canvas and handed it to Sandy Patty. "This is for you because you're my little sister. And I love ya." The painting actually took the little girl's breath away. "It's me!" she giggled. "And Lolly Polly. On the front porch. Look, everybody!"

Sam had painted his sister sitting cross-legged on the porch steps. Sandy Patty held a tiny pink dress in one hand and her doll in the other. It showed the little girl's yellow shorts and red top with flower shaped buttons. Her hair was pulled up into a curly, messy ponytail tied with a white ribbon. The faded blue-gray boards of the porch, with a red geranium plant sitting on one step, made a magical scene.

Next, Sam handed Miss Dove a canvas. Her hands shook as she took it from him, not expecting such a treasure. When she looked at it, she was stunned. It was her image, sitting on a bench in Middleton Park, surrounded by flowers. Sam had created an even more glorious flowerbed than was actually in the real park garden. Flowers of every color and size. It was a dazzling display. The best part was the gentle smile on the old woman's face.

"Sam! I can't thank you enough. What a wonderful painting and what a beautiful thought behind it. I *do* so love flowers."

It was Mr. Avery's turn. He was surprised when Sam handed him a canvas, too. What could it possibly be? It turned out to be something that touched the old man's heart. Mr. Avery recognized the backside of their house on Winslow Street. The ground was covered with yellow-, red-, and gold-colored leaves that had fallen from the trees. Someone was looking down from a third-story window to the gazebo below. It was him! When he looked closer at the gazebo, he could make out a figure sitting in front of an easel, painting a picture. The hat and white coat looked familiar. Noah! Sam had painted Mr. Avery looking down at his brother while he worked. It was almost too much for the old man to handle. He fumbled for his handkerchief and turned his back to the others.

"I hope ya like this," Sam told him. "It's kind of a thank you for all the supplies that you gave me. And it's a thanks to Noah, too, since it was his stuff that I used for these pictures. I'll never forget him and I'll never forget you, Mr. Avery."

Mr. Avery turned around and nodded at the little boy, still unable to say a word.

Sam picked up the last painting. He handed it to Chris. "This is for you, for all the nice things you do for us."

Chris saw himself sitting on their front porch steps, wearing his milkman's work shirt. But oddly enough, Sam had placed his mother sitting next to him. The couple appeared to be laughing at something. The wind had blown wisps of Annie's hair away from her face. Looking closer, it became clear that they were each holding some things. Dairy products! Cheese, a carton of milk, butter.

Chris held the canvas up so the others could see it. He looked at Annie, puzzled.

"Sam, why did you put me in Chris' picture?" his mother asked.

Sam seemed surprised. It had made sense to him. "Gee, Mom, he looked kind of lonely sitting there by himself. I thought if I put you in there too, he'd have some company."

* * *

CHAPTER 16
JUST A TRIM, PLEASE

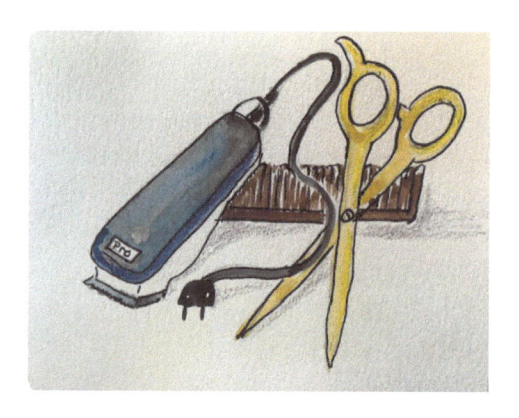

Mr. Avery knocked at the door of Number 101. When he'd gone out for his morning walk, he had discovered a package sitting outside the front door.

"Hi, Mrs. Cameron. Just found this on the porch. It's for Sam."

Annie dried her hands on her apron and took the box. "Sam, the stuff you ordered came."

He came racing out of his room. Sam had used up a lot of Noah's supplies, so he'd ordered some more online. He could well afford it with all the painting money he'd earned. As Sam sat at the table, rummaging through the box, Annie affectionately ruffled her son's hair.

"I wish we could order you a haircut online!" she said, laughing. "I swear, my children look like they're wearing mops on their heads."

"I could cut their hair."

Annie looked at the old man and grinned. "That's okay. I trim a little bit off every so often. Just enough to make them look presentable."

"I don't think you understand," Mr. Avery said. "Have you ever driven by Middleton Barber Shop that's next to the bank?" Annie nodded, not sure where he was going with this.

"That's my shop! That's what I did for years. Cut hair! Oh, sure, I've been retired for a while, but before this virus, I still had six employees working there. And when this crisis is over, I'll open it back up." He paused. "I'd love to cut some hair. I miss doing it."

"Are you sure you want to?" Annie asked. "I mean, it wouldn't be asking too much?"

"I don't know why I've never asked if anyone would like a haircut! Actually, I'd like to get back in action once in a while. Hey, what if I ask Miss Dove and Chris if they would like a trim later, too? I'll cut everybody's hair."

That evening they all gathered by the gazebo, with freshly washed hair. The first to go was Sam. Mr. Avery snipped and trimmed until Sam looked like a very good-looking young man. Then it was Sandy Patty's turn. Mr. Avery asked Annie if it was okay if he just trimmed the little girl's hair. "It's so pretty. It just needs a little bit cut off and she'll look wonderful," he told Annie. When he was finished, Sandy Patty hopped and skipped around the backyard, loving the feel of her crisp, bouncy curls.

Next, Miss Dove draped a towel around her shoulders and sat down in the chair they were using. "I feel like I just stepped into a story book beauty shop!" she laughed. "Why, getting a haircut out here among the trees and flowers feels like being in a fairy tale."

When Mr. Avery finished working on Miss Dove, he handed her a mirror.

"This looks fabulous! I feel so much better about my appearance. I guess I'll have to bake you something special in return."

"That would suit me just fine," Mr. Avery said, patting his stomach.

Then, it was Chris' turn. Mr. Avery snipped and trimmed, making the man look more handsome than ever. Finally, Annie sat down and waited for her haircut.

"Mrs. Cameron, do you want a lot taken off or just a little? Your hair has grown so long, it really looks beautiful. I can just trim the ends. Or I can cut more off. It's up to you."

"Just trim it," Chris blurted out.

Everyone looked at him.

"Oh, sorry! It'll look pretty, long or short. But it *is* beautiful a bit longer."

They all began to laugh at how embarrassed Chris was.

"Well, I guess I'll just have you trim the ends, Mr. Avery," Annie said with a smile. "And thanks for the compliment, Chris."

When Mr. Avery was done, she *did* look beautiful.

* * *

CHAPTER 17
ELEVENTY BILLION DOLLARS

Annie's cell phone rang and she pulled it out of her pocket. Who was calling?

"Hello," she answered.

"Mrs. Cameron?" a man asked. "My name is Red Miller. I'm the owner of Miller's Food Marts." Annie recognized the name of a big chain of grocery stores. Why was this business man calling her? "What can I do for you?" she asked.

"I got your number from Dr. Phillips, the medical director at St. Luke's Hospital there in Middleton. He's a friend of mine. He was telling me about the magnificent painting that your son, SamCam, did for the hospital." Mr. Miller sounded quite excited. "I'd like to talk to you both about a project I have in mind. Do you think your son would be interested in doing a piece that I could use in all my stores and advertisements? It would be a way of showing appreciation to all my employees and suppliers. They're the ones helping me keep the food available during this crisis. It's an important thank you campaign and I'm willing to pay him well for his art."

Annie took a deep breath. What was happening? Sam's work was getting noticed all over. He was becoming an artist of interest.

"Mr. Miller, I'll be happy to talk to my son about this. I'll call you back once we've discussed the matter."

"Please do! If SamCam is willing to help me out, I'll have my local manager bring you all the details. Why, this could be a major boost to his career! Your son is incredibly talented. I wouldn't mind buying some of his other original work, too."

Annie hung up and went looking for Sam. She found him playing horseshoes in the backyard with Sandy Patty and Chris. "Guess what, guys?" she called out. "Sam has another request for some of his artwork." Everyone stopped what they were doing and looked at her. She quickly told them what Mr. Miller had said. Sam's face lit up. Sandy Patty started dancing around in circles. Chris stared at Annie and his eyes got big. She nodded at him. This was an amazing offer. What should they do?

"That's a super idea!" Sam exclaimed.

"My brudder's an artist. My brudder's an artist," sang Sandy Patty.

The following day, Mr. L. J. Perkins, manager of the grocery stores, stopped at the house on Winslow Street. Annie had called Mr. Miller earlier and told him that Sam was willing to create artwork for his big thank you campaign. So, Mr. Perkins dropped off the information and supplies needed for the project. Annie examined the contract and then had Chris take it to her lawyer's office on his way to work. They both decided that the papers should be checked out first. Happily, her lawyer not only said that it was a wonderful opportunity—he was interested in buying some pieces of art, too!

Soon Sam was working hard. His thoughts were spinning as his paintbrush danced across the big canvas. Mr. Perkins had explained what Mr. Miller wanted on it and the little artist was delivering exactly what had been asked. What fun it was! Creating a piece of art was thrilling. He worked rapidly, completely lost in a world of colors.

It took twenty days to complete. There were so many details that made up the picture and Sam wanted everything to be just right. When Annie called Mr. Miller to tell him the work was finished, he was shocked. This was quicker than he had ever imagined. So, Annie took a picture of the canvas and texted it to him. She wanted to see if he thought it was what he had requested.

Twenty minutes later, a large car pulled up in front of the house. Mr. L. J. Perkins got out and stood on the sidewalk. "Hello, SamCam! Hello, Mrs. Cameron! Can you hear me?"

The family was in the middle of a game of Chinese Checkers at the kitchen table, but they stopped everything to run to the front door. Who was shouting?

When Mr. Perkins saw them, he waved excitedly. "Where's the painting? I can't wait to see it up close. Mr. Miller is thrilled and wanted me to pick it up as soon as possible."

Annie went into the house, got the large canvas, and leaned it against the porch steps. She stepped back inside the front door. Mr. Perkins sprinted up the sidewalk and stood gazing at it in delight.

"It's perfect. The faces of the employees and people who deliver our food stuffs are so realistic. The way the store front is shown is incredible. SamCam, you've created an excellent piece of art for our campaign." He stood shaking his head in disbelief that a little boy could produce such a vivid painting representing Miller's Food Marts. He looked closer. Ahh. In the lower right corner, there it was. SamCam. Mr. Perkins nodded in satisfaction.

"I was told to make sure that you had signed it. That was very important to Mr. Miller. Now, I'll leave a check with you. Uh, when Mr. Miller saw that photo you sent him, he decided to change the amount that we had agreed upon. I hope you'll be okay with the new amount." He took it from his jacket pocket and tucked it under the flower pot on the porch step. "Just remember, the more we use your image in our stores and ads, the more recognition you will be getting. In the future, my company may be needing more of your wonderful art."

After saying thank you several more times, Mr. Perkins put the painting in his car and drove off. Sandy Patty dashed over to the flower pot and got the check. Before she handed it to Sam, she squealed. "This one's gots lot of numbers. I think it says eleventy billion dollars!"

Annie looked over Sam's shoulder. "Well," she said slowly, "it's not exactly eleventy billion, but it's still mighty big. Ten thousand dollars! I can't believe it!" She quickly sat down on the steps.

Sam folded the check, handed it to his mother, and said, "I'd like to pay off our bills, if that's okay. We'll just save the rest. Now, let's get back to the game. I was winning, right?"

* * *

CHAPTER 18
TWO CONGRATULATIONS

Mr. Avery carried a platter of steaks to the picnic table in the backyard. He set it down next to a mac and cheese casserole, a basket of buttery rolls, and a steaming bowl of green beans. Miss Dove had made a three-layer chocolate cake with *CONGRATULATIONS* written across the top in white frosting. When they heard the rest of the group coming out the back door, they quickly stood next to each other to greet them.

"Surprise!"

Chris and the Camerons stopped. What was going on here? When Mr. Avery invited them for supper, Miss Dove had mysteriously told them not to bring anything but themselves. And now there was some kind of a surprise?

"Something smells dullicious," Sandy Patty declared.

"Is it somebody's birthday?" asked Sam.

Chris and Annie glanced at each other. They were as confused as the children.

"Well," Mr. Avery began, "you have all been invited here to celebrate two very important events. First, as we all know, Sam has accepted an important job with Miller's Food Marts. So, congratulations, young man."

Sam stepped forward and gave a comical little bow. "Thank you, thank you. I couldn't have done it without all of you!" he said, giggling.

Everyone clapped and whistled, then waited to hear what else the couple had to say.

"Miss Dove and I have become aware of something that the Camerons don't yet know about. We are also gathered here to celebrate a wonderful thing concerning Chris. It's come to our attention that our favorite milkman is no longer a milkman. He finished his college courses and received his degree. He's been promoted to Business Manager at the dairy company. So, congratulations to *you*, Chris."

All three Camerons turned to look at their friend. He hadn't said a word to them about it. Chris' face flushed a dull red shade. Sam reached out and shook his hand. Sandy Patty danced around in circles, chanting, "Chris got peemoted. Chris got peemoted." Annie threw her arms around him and gave him a big hug. "That's so wonderful! I'm very proud of you."

Chris grinned at her and then stepped back and, like Sam, gave a little comical bow. "Thank you, thank you. I couldn't have done it without all of you!" Everyone burst out laughing. Mr. Avery slapped his knee in delight.

"You know what?" Chris asked, as he looked down into Annie's eyes. "I think this is the best day ever!"

* * *

CHAPTER 19
MR. AVERY HAS AN IDEA

Things began to look up for everyone living in the Winslow Street house. The crazy virus continued on, but the world didn't seem so dark and gray. Maybe it was because Mr. Avery, Miss Dove, Chris, and the Camerons now realized that some of their most favorite people in the whole world all lived under the very same roof.

Annie could be heard humming happily as she dusted and swept Number 101. With help from her mother, Sandy Patty enjoyed baking treats for the others. Her specialty was smooshed cookies. Chris came home every afternoon from the office and the whole bunch spent some time on the front porch, telling each other how their day had gone. Sometimes Mr. Avery and Miss Dove entertained them with stories about the old days when they were young and the world had been so different.

And Sam began a comfortable schedule. He would paint as much as he wanted on the first four days of the week. On the fifth day he would concentrate on helping his mother around the house. Every sixth day he read or watched TV. Then, on the seventh day, he devoted all his time to playing with Sandy Patty. Which meant, also playing with Lolly Polly and her doll friends. Hmmm. But this routine was quiet and fulfilling.

Then, one day Mr. Avery happened to walk past the Camerons' open front door. Inside sat dozens and dozens of finished paintings. He stopped and stared in disbelief at all the canvases. Sam had apparently completed a huge collection.

That gave Mr. Avery an idea.

* * *

CHAPTER 20
PICTURE TAKING DAY

Sam put on a new shirt and jeans. He combed his hair. Next, he helped Sandy Patty strap on her dressy sandals. He seemed quite calm about everything that was happening today.

Annie smoothed the front of her dress and patted her hair nervously. She looked out the window. White easels had been set up on the front lawn. Mr. Avery had arranged for Tim Tabor, Noah's old business manager, to hire a photographer to take pictures of Sam's collection. Some of the canvases were already placed on the easels. After each shot, different ones would be displayed so more pictures could be taken. The paintings were going to be sold during a live online auction and the photographs would be used to display his work.

"Are you sure you want to do this, Sam?" Annie asked.

Sam looked at his mother with a crooked little grin. "Mom, we're running out of space here. We both know I don't want to stop painting. So, the only smart thing to do is to sell some and share them with others. It doesn't bother me at all. I kept my favorites. I'm happy with that."

Annie smiled and shook her head. "For someone who is only nine years old, you sound like a wise, old man. Okay. Whatever you say."

"I can't wait until WMPT gets here for the intervoo," Sandy Patty suddenly chirped. "Maybe I'll get to be on TV!"

Annie's stomach churned. She was very nervous that the local TV station was coming to talk to them as they filmed the canvases set out on the lawn. Word had gotten around town that the little artist who had created so many uplifting paintings lived on Winslow Street. Everyone was curious about the young boy who had suddenly showed an amazing talent almost overnight. Several of his famous thank you paintings were displayed around town. But many of his other works hadn't been seen before. Now, everyone wanted to get a look at them, too.

When the TV crew showed up, they set their camera in place to film the photographer snapping pictures for Sam's exhibit. They did close-ups on many of the paintings and everyone was oohing and ahhhing. "Testing! Testing!" the director said into the microphone before he attached it to a long pole and aimed it toward the Camerons.

The interview went well, even though Sandy Patty felt the need to go into her spinning around act right next to Sam. Annie silently took her hand and led her out of the camera's view.

When the reporter questioned Sam how he had gotten started, he spoke honestly. "It just came to me. Even my mom asked me how I could do this without lessons. I don't know. For years, I watched my neighbor, Noah Avery. He made it look so easy. Then one day I decided to paint a thank you sign for our yard. And that was the beginning."

"I understand that you may be doing something interesting with some of the money you earn from your auction. Can you tell us about that?'"

Sam frowned. "I'm not sure how you found out about that, but, yup, I want to give some to the Middleton Food Bank. My mom has always taken good care of my sister and me, but I don't want other kids to go hungry. Nobody likes to be hungry. Food is important to get grown up."

After the interview was over, Tim Tabor smiled. "You all did a wonderful job. I especially liked Sandy Patty's dance routine." He winked at the little girl. "And, Sam, you were remarkable. I'm very proud to be representing you for your auction. This TV coverage will give you lots of advertisement for the sale. Anyone who ends up with one of your paintings is going to feel very lucky."

Chris came walking up the sidewalk just as Tim was leaving. He sat down next to Annie on the porch swing. She didn't think a bit about social distancing as long as they wore their masks. She was just so glad to see him after her stressful day. He took her hand. "I watched everything from the sidewalk. It went great. You should all be proud of yourselves. *You*, Little Missy," he said pointing to Sandy Patty. "That was the best twirling around I've ever seen." The little girl giggled and put her hands over her face. "Sam," he continued, "you handled yourself so well. And it's wonderful that you're willing to share with others. The food bank is a terrific idea!"

"As for you," he said, turning to Annie, "I couldn't believe how beautiful you looked. Wow, you stayed so calm."

"Thank you. But I didn't feel very calm."

Sandy Patty and Sam watched the couple sitting together on the swing. Chris was gently holding their mother's hand! Sandy Patty's eyes got big. She began to smile. Then she began to giggle, again. She gave her brother a thumbs up! Sam saw how happy his mother was with Chris. Suddenly, he felt a warm, glad feeling in his chest. He began to grin, and flashed a big thumbs up right back at his sister. *This* was the best day ever.

* * *

CHAPTER 21
MUM'S THE WORD

"Whew! I'm glad that's over!" Annie pushed the computer screen away and stood up. It had been a month since the TV interview, and now the live online auction was finally over.

"SamCam," she teased, "how do you feel about selling every single one of your paintings? I'll bet that's some kind of record."

The Camerons and Chris had spent the afternoon watching the auction together in the living room. It had been interesting and exciting, but they were all relieved when it was done.

Sam looked happy. "I think it's great. Now we have the space so I can paint more pictures. Boy, do I have a lot of ideas," he said.

Sandy Patty put her little hands on her hips. "All the other pictures were bootiful, but I still think you did the bestest job with the one of me and Lolly Polly. I had Mommy hang it in my room so I can look at it every day."

"Hey!" Annie pretended to pout. "I think *my* picture of the sunflowers with the secret message is the best."

"Wait! The one of your mother and me is the best," declared Chris.

"Thanks," Sam said, "but you guys are all right. I tried to do the best for each one of you. What you think about them is what really matters."

Just then, Annie's phone rang. She listened to what the caller was saying and then burst out, "What? Oh, my goodness! Really? Call me back when you get all the details."

Three pairs of eyes were watching her.

"What's up?" Chris asked.

"Nothing," said Annie smugly. "Nothing at all."

"Tell us!" begged Sandy Patty.

"Nope. It's a surprise. A big surprise! You are just going to have to wait and see."

No matter what the other three said, she wouldn't tell them. They began to tickle her but she just laughed. They would just have to wait!

*   *   *

CHAPTER 22
A LITTLE HERO

Annie came into the living room, looking for her children.

"Sam, how would you and Sandy Patty like to go for a ride in the car?" she asked, casually. "We haven't been out in quite a while. It might do us good to see if there's anything going on downtown."

Sam's head jerked up from the book he was reading. "Yippee!" he shouted

"Yippee, yippee, yippee!" Sandy Patty joined in.

Annie clapped her hands together. "Alright, kiddos. Go get cleaned up and put on some fresh clothes. We're goin' downtown."

Neither one of the children stopped to ask what had brought this on. They hadn't been out for a car ride in a long time. But it didn't matter. They were just excited about doing something different.

When Sam was ready, he went out on the front porch to wait for the others. How surprised he was to see Mr. Avery, Miss Dove, and Chris there.

"What's going on?" he asked.

"Nothing," said Mr. Avery.'

"Not a thing," answered Chris.

"Oh, we're just sitting out here watching the world go by," Miss Dove replied.

This was odd. Chris usually tidied up his apartment on Saturdays, Miss Dove always took her nap at this time, and Mr. Avery watched his favorite afternoon TV shows. Just then, Annie and Sandy Patty came out of the house.

"Why, hello everyone," Annie said, winking at them. "We're going for a little ride around town. I hope you have a nice time sitting here on the porch."

All three porch sitters waved their hands and called out good byes. As Annie drove off, Sam looked back and noticed something really odd. His porch sitting friends had jumped to their feet and were heading for Chris's car. He shrugged. They were acting a little strange today, but he was too busy looking out the window and seeing Middleton again. It was fun driving by the homes of some of his schoolmates. His friend, Joey Sims, was actually out in his front yard. Sam rolled down his window and shouted a hello as Annie drove by.

"Hi, Sam!" Joey yelled back. "Hey, I'll see ya later!"

Sam was confused. "Mom, did you hear Joey say he'd see me later? What's that mean? We both know we can't play together yet."

"Hmmm," Annie said, "I have no idea what he was talking about." She had a hard time keeping a smile off her face.

Down one street and up another. It was great to ride past the pretty creek that was on the edge of town, then go by the school and downtown stores. Suddenly, Sam noticed that he was seeing a lot of people walking along the sidewalks. Everyone wore masks as they walked six feet apart. It looked like a long, winding parade. And several cars were driving toward the center of town!

Finally, Annie headed to the town square and found a space for the car in the crowded parking lot. They spotted a stage decorated with strings of twinkling lights. A man stood behind a podium which held a microphone. Lots and lots of people had gathered on the grassy area, all standing apart. It seemed like the whole town was here. Everyone acted like they were waiting for something.

"Let's get out and see what's going on," Annie told the children. "Remember, social distancing!" As they walked toward the center of the town square, the crowd moved apart, making a wide path so the Camerons could walk forward. Sam looked around. He recognized so many people. Then he saw Mr. Avery, Miss Dove, and Chris at the edge of the crowd! What were they doing here? And wait! He saw Joey with his parents. Why, there were lots of his other school friends here, too.

At this time Mr. Gibbs, the mayor of Middleton, stepped up to the microphone. "Attention, everyone! Our guest of honor has arrived." When everyone turned in Sam's direction, he turned, too. He couldn't understand what they were looking at. Annie leaned down and whispered something in his ear.

"This is for *you*, Son."

His eyes got wide as he stared up at his mother.

"For what?" he whispered back.

"Samuel Cameron! Or, should I say SamCam?" the mayor called out. "Would you please come a little closer to the stage?"

As Sam walked forward, everyone began to clap for him. Sandy Patty didn't know what was going on either, but she began hopping up and down in all the excitement. The applause got louder and louder.

"Ladies and gentlemen. We are here today to recognize a wonderful member of our community. He lives with his mother and sister on Winslow Street and is only nine years old. He has brilliantly shared his artistic talent to thank our fellow citizens who take care of us all. His work is a joy to look at and has thrilled the hearts of so many. His intention was to honor the heroes among us, but he has also been uplifting to *everyone* in Middleton." Mr. Gibbs looked out at the large crowd. "So, today, we wish to honor *him* for all the goodwill he has shared with this town. This young man has encouraged others to stand tall and strong during this crisis. This young man has generously realized the importance of others in our community. This young man is a hero himself!"

The mayor nodded to some men standing in front of a huge canvas curtain. They cut the rope ties, the curtain fell away, and a big metal sign mounted on a large marble slab revealed the following message:

MIDDLETON WISHES TO HONOR
SAMUEL CAMERON
FOR ALL HIS BEAUTIFUL ART THAT IS
SO INSPIRING TO OUR COMMUNITY.
THANK YOU "SAMCAM",
THE HERO FROM WINSLOW STREET.

* * *

CHAPTER 23
THE VERY, VERY, VERY BEST DAY EVER!

Sam Cameron opened the door of the big house on Winslow Street and headed out to the front porch. It was early in the evening, and the cool, crisp air felt wonderful on his face. He'd come out here to sit on the porch steps and think. Sam had a lot to think about.

He was so happy to finally see his grandparents again. His mom's parents and his dad's parents had come to see them. Two uncles, one aunt, and three cousins were also here. Everyone got to meet Chris's parents, too! They'd all gathered for a special social-distancing get-together.

Sam thought about how pretty his sister and mother looked today. Sandy Patty had on a fluffy pink dress and her hair was done up in a swirl of curls. Mom wore a dress that was the palest blue color he had ever seen. He couldn't wait to use that shade in some of his paintings.

Sam looked down at his black pants and shiny dress shoes. He and Chris were dressed just alike. That was really fun. It made Sam feel so grown-up.

And the cake! It was the most elegant thing that Sam had ever seen. Miss Dove had made it especially for today. It was so tasty he had already eaten three pieces.

The wedding had gone perfectly. Chris and Annie had finally figured out that they couldn't live without each other. That made everyone very happy, especially Mr. Avery and Miss Dove. The sun was shining on the happy couple as they joined hands in the decorated gazebo. Sam and Sandy Patty stood proudly by their sides while they exchanged their vows.

After the ceremony Grandma and Grandpa Cameron made a surprising announcement. Since Chris was leaving his small apartment and moving into Number 101 with Annie and the children, they had decided to rent Number 202 so they could live closer to the family. Everyone was excited about that. Mr. Avery and Miss Dove looked at each other and nodded. Perhaps the older Camerons would like to get together for a game of cards sometime. Having even more friends in the house on Winslow Street would be a blessing.

Suddenly, Sam's thoughts were interrupted by the sound of the screen door opening. Chris came out and sat down on the porch steps next to him. He put his arm around the little boy. "Are you having a good time today? I am."

Sam took Chris's hand, gave it a little squeeze and then leaned his head against the man's shoulder. "You know what, Chris? It's not just Mom. Sandy Patty and I love you, too."

"And I love *you* guys so much!" Chris said in a shaky voice.

"You know what else, Chris?" Sam stood up. He began to shout in the loudest voice he could manage, so everyone would hear. "*THIS IS THE VERY, VERY, VERY BEST DAY EVER!*"

Annie came hurrying out of the house, followed by the others. "Is everything okay? I heard someone yelling!"

Sam and Chris looked at each other and burst out laughing. Annie looked from one to the other and then back again. Then she began to chuckle and soon everyone else joined in. Sam grabbed Sandy Patty's hand and ran with her across the yard, shouting his happy message over and over again.

Chris stood up and put his arm around his new bride. "No matter how awful the world seems right now, if we hold on to each other and those wonderful children, every day will seem like the very, very, very best day ever!"

As she took his hand and pulled him out into the yard to join all the others, she looked up into his eyes. "I couldn't agree more."

* * *

CHAPTER 24
A FAMILY PORTRAIT

His latest painting was finished! Of course, it was signed SamCam. Grandpa Cameron had helped him get it professionally framed. If ever Sam had a favorite piece of work, this was it. Everyone he dearly loved was in it.

    He listened to the chatter that flowed through an open window from the front porch. Soon, he would have them all gather in the living room to see it. The love he felt for his mother, sister, Chris, grandparents, Miss Dove, and Mr. Avery showed in every brush stroke he'd made. Sam had even put Chip, their new dog, right smack dab in the front of everyone. Chip had been a gift from Chris, and the entire family adored him.

Sam smiled. This picture showed little special things about all of them. He wondered how long it would take before all the quirky stuff would be noticed. He had painted a sunflower lying on Annie's lap. Chris had one arm around his new wife's shoulder while holding a melting ice cream cone in his hand. Sandy Patty had Lolly Polly perched on her shoulder. There was a pair of hair clippers tucked into Mr. Avcry's suit jacket pocket and Miss Dove was holding a decorated cake. Grandma and Grandpa Cameron both wore fishing hats because they loved to fish. Annie's parents, who liked to read, each held a small stack of books. Sam stood to the side of everyone with a paint brush in one hand and a huge grin on his face. Chip was proudly sitting right up front with a chewed-up slipper in his mouth. He looked like he was grinning, too.

Finally, Sam had included a message for all his loved ones and anyone else who saw this picture. Painted at the bottom of the canvas was this:

HAVE FAITH THAT THESE TIMES CAN GET BETTER AND THEY WILL

The End

Dedications and Acknowledgements

I would like to dedicate this little book to my daughter, **Jenna Ahmann**. Your patience and willingness to help, as you dragged me into the 21st century and taught me the basic functions of the computer, made this book possible. Thankfully, your confidence in me as a story teller has never wavered. I love you.

And

Sister No. 3, **Judith Schatzle** (also a children's book author) who has always believed in me. She's been there to read my rough drafts and to push me forward. Thanks, Jude, from me, Sister No. 4.

And mostly

Sister No. 2, the late **Sandra Harms**, aka Puppet Master, who would constantly call me over the years and demand to know if I had written anything that day. She was my guiding light and toughest critic, and I miss her so much.

> Note: There *is* a sister No. 1, **Karen Frerick**, but she is not interested in the writing business, so I'll just say thanks for encouraging me to read, read, read from the time I was a youngster. That, alone, is a big deal.

My sincere thanks to the talented, award-winning author, and my editor, **Rosemary J. Fisher**, for welcoming me into her circle of writers, and for working so hard to make this book a wonderful experience. I am having so much fun! I can't express how much she has altered the next chapter of my life. I look forward to reading all of *her* future work, too. It is interesting that Mrs. Fisher began her novel writing after retiring from her career as a teacher. You go, Girl!

Much appreciation to the incredible artist, **Cris Sell**, for creating such a beautiful book cover. His skills and imagination are unmatched and his enthusiasm in being involved in SamCam's story was a gift. Much like the young boy in the book, Mr. Sell's artistic talents took off suddenly…after he retired from a career as a mechanical engineer. His works of art are true gems.

A huge thank you to **Deb Weiser**, artist, teacher, and owner of the **dkwgallery**, and her students, **Sam Dlomme**, **Lily Juergens**, **Lee Grooms**, and **Hayden Schultz**, who created the imaginative chapter illustrations. Their talents show so strongly in the whimsical, creative, and heartfelt ideas they came up with for this book. I predict much bigger things for them in their artistic future!

And THANK YOU to **Lora Monroe** and her **team** from **Writers' Branding** for their patience, kindness, and hard work on this project.

***

Janene Oliphant is also the author of
The Adventures of Molly and Pet.